FIRE IN THE FOREST!

By Samantha Brooke
Illustrated by Kenny Kiernan

SCHOLASTIC INC.

NEW YORK   TORONTO   LONDON   AUCKLAND

SYDNEY   MEXICO CITY   NEW DELHI   HONG KONG

ISBN 978-0-545-36992-3

LEGO, the LEGO logo, the Brick and Knob configurations and the Minifigure are trademarks of the LEGO Group. © 2012 The LEGO Group. Produced by Scholastic Inc. under license from the LEGO Group.

All rights reserved. Published by Scholastic Inc. SCHOLASTIC and associated logos are trademarks and/or registered trademarks of Scholastic Inc.

Lexile is a registered trademark of MetaMetrics.

12 11 10 9 8 7 6

Designed by Angela Jun
Printed in the U.S.A.
First printing, January 2012

12 13 14 15 16 17/0

40

The firemen are inside the firehouse in the forest. It is a quiet day.

Then the fire alarm rings.
"Wake up! I see smoke!" says Ted.

Ben does not want to get out of bed.

The firemen slide down the pole. "Look out!"

The firefighters get into the fire truck.

They zoom through the forest. "Hold on, Ben!"

"Where is the fire?" asks Ted.
"Right here," says a camper.

"This is not a forest fire," says Ben. "It is a campfire."

"Got to go!" says Ben.

The firemen try to put out the fire.
But the fire does not stop.

There is a lot of smoke.
The firefighters can not see.
"Who turned out the lights?" asks
Ben.

The firemen call for help.

The fire plane will help put out the fire.

"Look!"
Here comes the fire plane.

The plane drops water on the fire.

The firemen get wet, too.

Ben gets the fire hose.
The water comes out fast.
Woah!

"We have one more stop to make," says Ben.

Then they will return to the firehouse.

"Hard work makes me hungry!" says Ben.

BUILD YOUR LEGO® LIBRARY!

■SCHOLASTIC

www.scholastic.com
www.LEGO.com

LEGOC